PROTECTION

PROTECTION

TT Kove

Protection
by TT Kove

Published by Arctic Circle Press
Cover designed by Tina T. Kove

Edited by Tami Veldura

All rights reserved. No part of this book may be used or reproduced in any manner without written permission, except for in the purpose of reviews.

This book is a work of fiction and as such all characters and situations are fictitious. Any resemblance to actual people, place, or events is coincidental.

First edition July 2015.
Copyright © 2015 by TT Kove
www.ttkove.com

About the story

Adrian isn't looking for a boyfriend. He's focused on school and social situations make him anxious. When his mother encourages him to make a friend and be more outgoing, he takes a chance at a party. It doesn't live up to expectations. His classmates ignore him and the alcohol tastes bad. Worse? Oliver finds him moping in the bathroom.

Oliver, the class clown and know-it-all, might grate Adrian's last nerve, but he's the only one paying Adrian any attention. Not only does Oliver flirt him into a bedroom, he charms Adrian's pants off. Adrian loses his virginity to a man he doesn't even like and in the morning his anxiety spirals into full panic. They didn't use protection and popular-with-everyone Oliver insists they need to get tested.

Adrian is sure this isn't the kind of friendship his mother meant and he tries to distance himself. But it turns out Oliver's brash personality is just a mask to hide his own insecurities and family embarrassments. Adrian can relate. Oliver may be a know-it-all, yet Adrian can't abandon him. Besides, they still need their test results. But how can the popular kid be friends with him when Adrian doesn't want to come out of his shell?

Chapter One

I hate parties.

I hovered by the door leading into the living room. It was crowded with people drunk off their arses. They looked, quite frankly, ridiculous the way they tried to flirt and hook up with each other. It was disgusting. *No one had better come over to me with their cheesy pick-up lines.*

I wanted to leave. But the front door was on the opposite side of the living room. To get there I had to cross said room full of people who would *notice* me. Not that anyone had spoken to me yet since I arrived, but I *had* been invited. Probably because I'd been within earshot when my classmates had been talking about it, but I had been asked nonetheless.

Why did I say yes?

That was the million dollar question. I didn't like parties, I didn't like being sociable. I wasn't good at it. Drawing attention to myself... I couldn't do it.

People headed for the kitchen, almost shouting at each other to be heard over the music and everyone else.

I drew back and turned to find somewhere to hide.

My gaze fell on a door that had a simple WC sign on it. *Really?* What was the point of that in their own house? That was the kind of sign for public toilets. Maybe that was the point.

Still, it was a room. A door with a lock.

I could hide in there until the party calmed down and I dared to venture into that living room. *I did this for you, Mum.* I opened the door and found the room empty. I breathed a sigh in relief. *You wanted me to be sociable and here I am. Never again.* Never ever. This was the last time I tried. Being cooped up in my room was heaven compared to this.

I closed the door after me. A bottle clinked against the wood. I looked down at my other hand and the beer bottle clutched in it. I'd forgot about it in my panic facing the living room. Someone had pressed it into my hand when I'd arrived.

I crossed the small room to lean against the smooth wall, slowly sinking down to sit on the floor.

I should go home and enjoy my own company. Get on the laptop and get online. Play a game, do coursework, anything else but sitting here hiding. I didn't even have my sketchbook with me, so I couldn't draw. I could do that at home though.

I sat the bottle of beer on the floor next to me. I eyed it. I had drunk from it and it had tasted like piss. Not that I knew what that tasted like, but it was what I imagined it *would* taste like. I hadn't ever drunk alcohol—never felt the need to. Not having any mates or being sociable meant I'd never experienced any peer pressure.

Tonight was, apparently, a night for new adventures though. I took another sip of the vile thing and almost choked as a result. I forced it down on sheer willpower. Perhaps tonight was the night I would experience being drunk. It wouldn't take long if I got the beer down. Not being used to alcohol, I wouldn't need much to feel the effects. Or so the internet told me. Why anyone liked beer, or would drink it to savour the taste, was beyond me.

I drank some more. Torturing myself was what I was doing. I should leave, but then I'd have to go through the living room where everyone was gathered. I couldn't do that. I couldn't risk having all their attention on me—it would definitely leave me in a state of panic.

Slam!

I looked up, startled. A bloke had slipped

inside, closed the door after him, and now he blinked down at me. He had unruly blond hair with a fringe falling over his forehead and into his eyes. It was like he'd just got out of bed—but it was quite deliberately done. He had wide, brown eyes. I hadn't known they were brown, but then I never made a habit of studying him either. He was dressed in loose-fitting jeans, black Converse trainers, and a tight, black jumper, with a red T-shirt over it. There was no denying he looked *good*. Still...

Gad. I wanted to groan, but managed to keep it in. Of all people I could end up in a bathroom with, it had to be *him*.

"Sorry, didn't mean to barge in on you." He turned around to leave again. His fingers wrapped around the handle, ready to press it down.

"It's all right." I bowed my head to stare down at my beer bottle. What was I doing? Encouraging him to stay? What in the world was I doing that for?

He sunk to the floor and rested his back against the door. "Not in a party mood?"

I shook my head in the negative. *Why'd I stop him from leaving? Why's he making conversation with me?*

"Me neither." He rested his hands over his

knees as he looked around curiously. "You had too much to drink?"

I shook my head again. Apparently I'd gone mute. I swallowed the last of the beer, grimacing as I did so. "It doesn't taste any good."

He chuckled. "You got to get used to it. Only one beer, though? You won't be feeling tipsy with that. How about we go get some more and find a more comfortable place to drink them?"

I cast him an askew glance. "You drunk?" It was hard to tell, what with him being quite talkative on a normal day. *In class, anyway.*

"Not yet." He grinned. "But I plan to be."

Of course he did. "Why?" Yes, why indeed. Why was I having a conversation with him? I should get up and leave. Right this instant. But I didn't.

"Because I've had a shit day and I just want to forget about it for a while." He shrugged, as if chasing bad thoughts away with alcohol was a regular, safe way to deal with bad things. *Maybe for him it is.*

Then again, forgetting for a while did sound like a good idea.

For the first time in my life I decided to be impulsive. Well, second, since I *had* said yes to this dreadful party. I stood up and stared down at him, stomach churning in anxiety, but my mind made up. "You coming?"

"Yeah." He scrambled up off the floor and opened the door. Together we went to the kitchen. It felt a lot safer going there with someone else. *Even him.* I threw my old bottle out, though it didn't seem like anyone else bothered with it. Well, at least I wasn't being a slob and contributing to the mess that had to be cleaned up by whoever owned this flat in the morning.

He took a six-pack from the fridge before turning to me. "Let's go find somewhere quiet."

I silently followed him. *Why, though? I don't like him, so I shouldn't be going anywhere with him.* But I kept following him.

He glanced into a couple rooms we passed, and though I didn't look inside them, the sounds couldn't be mistaken. He entered the last room. It was dark, but he switched the light on before heading further inside. I looked around from the doorway, taking in the plain, simple room. *Bed*room, to be exact. With a wide double bed. It was made, thankfully, which meant someone hadn't been in here to do— whatever they felt like doing.

"Lock the door." He dropped onto the bed where he sat watching me.

I did as told, simply out of surprise, then

slowly approached the bed. What did he think was going to happen? Were we supposed to sit here and chat like we were old mates?

"I'm Oliver, by the way." He said this as he struggled getting the beer out of the package. When he had one beer free, he handed it to me.

"Adrian." I knew his name. He was in my language class, after all. He obviously didn't seem to know mine though. *Invisible*. That's what I was. That was me. The Invisible Man. I could totally be a superhero if that was my calling. "Do you have an opener?" I had no idea how to open beer bottles without one.

"Don't need one of those." When I simply stared at him, he reached out for the bottle. "Let me do it." Once I handed it over, he opened the top with his teeth before handing it back to me. Once rid of it, he leant back on his hand and took a long swig from his own. "So why're you here if you're not in the mood for it?"

"Why're *you* here?" I didn't want to tell him, so I brought the question around on him instead. He loved answering questions, after all. "You're not in the mood either."

"I told you: I want to get drunk." He held his bottle up, tilted it towards me a bit like we were toasting. "So here I am, beer at hand, and locked in a bedroom getting pissed off of it." He looked at me inquiringly now. "So why're you here?"

I shrugged. "Some classmates asked me to be here."

"But they're not *here* with you. Shitty classmates then."

Or I was the shit one, perhaps. They'd been nice, inviting me. Or maybe they'd just done so because I'd been sitting there, right next to them when they chatted about it? Maybe they didn't want me here at all. Maybe they didn't know my name either.

Silence stretched out between us. I didn't mind so much, I liked silence. I wasn't much for conversation, anyway. Scared of saying something wrong or weird. I reckon he didn't though — he seemed to always be speaking whenever I was around to hear him.

New beers were opened once we finished the ones we'd been drinking. I was getting light-headed. The room spun a bit. I didn't even taste the flavour anymore. I felt relaxed, more *loose*. I was never loose, I was always bound tight. A tight ball of anxiety.

Oliver scooted close to me. I glanced at him, curious. He grinned, then his lips mashed against mine in a hard kiss. I stiffened. *Bloody hell! I don't want to kiss him!* My body betrayed me and relaxed against him. I kissed him *back*. I hadn't ever kissed anyone before, but kissing felt *good*. The hard kiss moved into a softer one.

His hands slid up my arms to lock tightly around my neck. He pressed himself against me. My arms lifted of their own accord, certainly not with any permission from me, to grip the back of his tee. *Oh shit.*

He moaned softly against my lips and that sound went straight through any reservations I had. It was hard to take that sound for anything but what it was. So was the kiss, for that matter. The tip of his tongue ran over my lips. I panicked silently, not at all sure I wanted someone else's tongue in my mouth, but he parted my lips and it was *there*. His tongue slid against mine, teasing me. Our saliva mixed. I wasn't sure how I felt about that. Initial reaction was *eww*, but... it felt kind of nice.

I gripped him tighter. He was all hard and warm. Definitely a man's body. *Who knew it would feel so good to just be this close to another man*. One of his hands tangled in my hair. The other slid down my chest. He slipped it under the hem of my jumper, ran it up my chest again. My whole body thrummed in response to that soft, warm hand caressing me.

He pulled back suddenly. Before sense could return to me, he pulled his T-shirt and jumper off. He threw them to the floor without so much as a care to where they landed.

My gaze zeroed in on his chest, his stomach, and stopped where his bare skin met the denim of his jeans. *Oh fuck*. He was hard—I could see the ridge of his— cock—pressing against the material. I shuddered as I realised that I too was affected by *him*, and I was about to panic all over again when he reached down to unbutton and unzip his jeans.

A heavy swallow was all I could manage. My gaze now zeroed in on the thin, white pants revealed. The head of his—well, cock—was clearly outlined through it. My mouth went dry. *Shit. What am I about to do? How do I do this?*

"Fuck me," he whispered against my lips.

I couldn't move. Couldn't say anything. This was too much, too soon. I'd never done anything like this before—and I'd never wanted to. Not until now, apparently. I had wondered what it would be like, of course, but never met anyone I could even imagine doing it with.

He reached for my jeans and deftly unzipped me. Now my swallow was audible, as witness by his sudden grin. I was so nervous. I might either explode or bolt. His hand slid down the front of my boxers, cupping me in the palm of his hand. My pulse sped up rapidly. Never had I felt anything like the sensation shooting through me at someone else's hand on my junk. It felt so *good*.

He tried to get us both out of our jeans, but he struggled. I pushed his hands gently away from me. "I'll do it," I mumbled, not meeting his eyes.

I slowly pulled my jeans off, leaving the pants on. When I dared cast a glance at him he was already naked and stretching out on the bed. He stared at my groin for a second, then sat up straight and reached for my waist. He pulled me close.

He leaned in, then paused and glanced up as if he was asking for permission. *He's going to go down on me*. That thought flashed in my mind, like a great big sign. He pulled my boxers down, wrapped one hand around my erection, and stroked it a couple times. Up, the foreskin covered the mushroom head. Down, revealing the mushroom head in all its glory. He leant in further, lips wrapping around the head, sliding down until he'd taken me in all the way.

Oh gad. I'd read about it, seen it in porn—though I didn't watch that often. He was deep-throating me. He must be experienced if he could do that. Not that I was that big, but I didn't think I was that small either. I would never be able to do what he did, for sure. *Oh!* Gasps left me and I tilted my head back at the sensations made from his mouth on my—cock. It felt so dirty thinking that. He started sucking. *Bloody hell.* It was like nothing I'd ever felt before. So intense. So *amazing*.

Then he left me dry as he pulled off and fell back on the bed. I stared down at him, quizzical, until he put two fingers in his own mouth. He sucked on them and they came out wet with saliva. He moved his hand down his body and he hitched one leg up. His fingers slid down his crack and over his hole. He seemed to be teasing it for a bit, then one finger penetrated.

I stared. I couldn't help it. I'd only ever seen this in porn, and there it was usually the other partner doing this. In real-life, however, and witnessing how he worked himself… I'd never imagined this before. It was captivating. Maybe I'd had a peek at the wrong kind of porn.

"Get the rest of your clothes off." His voice was low and husky.

I blushed at the request, realising I was standing in front of the bed, erection pointing upwards, boxers around my thighs, my jumper still on. *I must look ridiculous.* I slid the boxers down my legs and kicked them off to where I'd dropped my jeans. My jumper and T-shirt came next. Once I was as naked as he was, I tentatively put a trembling knee on the bed. I watched him with wide eyes.

He had two fingers in himself now. In, out, in, out, in quick succession. His pupils were blown, his gaze filled with the pleasure he was inducing on himself. Not that I could ever imagine it would feel pleasurable to insert something down there, but to each his own.

"I want your cock." He eyed said appendage.

I, in turn, eyed his fingers, the way they slid so easily into him. Two fingers were fine, but an erect cock? I wasn't that big—I didn't think anyway, certainly a lot smaller than the blokes in porn—but I reckoned it would hurt. It wasn't like we had the big tubes of lube always lying around in porn.

He pulled his fingers out. His hole contracted once it wasn't being penetrated. He reached up to put a third finger in his mouth, getting that one all wet too, before inserting all three into himself. His eyes closed, his hole seemed to struggle with all three fingers, but then it gave way and he pressed them in as far as he could get them.

"Get up here." He'd opened his eyes again now and were looking at me. "I'm going to suck you, get you all wet, and then you're going to fuck me."

"But—"

"Come on." He motioned with his free hand and I scooted closer. How was this going to work? He was on his back, pleasuring himself. It wasn't like he could lean over me again. "Straddle me."

Slowly, very slowly, I did as he said. I straddled his shoulders, pushed my groin forward, and he lifted his head. "You fuck my mouth, okay?"

What? But when his lips wrapped around my head, my hips seemed to move of their own accord. I moved slow, because honestly, if I moved any quicker how could that be good for him?

He made a sound in the back of his throat, then his hand cupped my bum, squeezing. He pushed me forward harder, showing me exactly how he wanted it. I matched it and then his hand landed on my thigh instead.

It was messy, no doubt about that. His mouth was open around me as I— well, as I fucked his mouth. Saliva trickled down both sides of his mouth, as well as gathering around me. I could feel the wetness, could feel how slippery I was.

He pushed my hips back and managed to wriggle around onto his stomach while I still straddled his shoulders. I got off quickly and saw him reach over his bum now, inserting those three fingers again. He moaned.

"Come on. Get in me. *Now*."

I scrambled down, gaze practically glued to his hole. It didn't seem to mind those three fingers at all, taking it all easily. He glanced at me over his shoulder. When he saw me in place, he pulled his fingers out. He brought them under himself to wrap around his bobbing erection instead.

I moved in closer, hands clamping down on his hips. He spread his legs wider, bum pushing back against me. I had to release one side of his hips to guide my cock to his hole, because it didn't seem to want to go in without some help. I held it fast. Aimed at his hole. Pushed forward. *Just like they do in porn.* His hole fought me. *Not like it happens in porn.* It didn't want to let me in, but he helped by pushing against me, and then... I was inside.

He groaned. A groan of pain. I could hear it and see how he struggled. I wanted to pull back, but he was still pushing his bum towards me. He was still taking me further in. I bit down on my lip to keep any sounds threading to escape inside. It was too intense, too tight, but so bloody *good*. He squeezed around my cock.

Voluntary or not, I didn't know. The pleasure it brought to be so snug was unbelievable.

He was panting heavily—and to my horror, so was I. It didn't seem to matter anymore though, to keep my voice inside, because I was inside *him*. That was all my body cared about and my brain short-circuited.

It was too much too soon. I came—sputtering sperm inside him, my whole body shuddering at the quick and intense orgasm. I collapsed to his side, on my back as he had been earlier. I put my hands over my face to hide it, which must be completely red now. I hadn't even lasted long enough to thrust properly.

He flipped around, moaned more as he furiously stroked himself. His fingers were back inside him. His eyes were closed. He worked himself so well, completely at tune with his body. He knew what he wanted, knew what he liked, and he didn't shy away from doing it. His hips bucked up against his hand. His moans were getting loader. My eyes widened as sperm shot out of the head of his cock. It landed on his stomach, his groin, and some on the sheets. *Oh gad.* He kept on stroking through the first splurge and more came to trickle down his length.

A loud sigh left him as he released his cock

and pulled his fingers out of his arse. His chest heaved, sweat drops glistening on it. His chest was completely smooth, so different from mine that had a smattering of dark, coarse hairs. I didn't know if he was smooth by nature or if he shaved. Then again... My gaze travelled down his body. His groan was trimmed too, so he probably shaved both places.

He grabbed for my hand, the one on my other side, so he had to scoot in close and fumble his hand over my chest. Once he got a hold of it, he squeezed and brought it around his shoulder. He moved onto his side, and I had to do so too as he tugged my arm around his waist. His breathing evened out. He was falling asleep. I was drowsy too, my eyelids suddenly had a hard time keeping themselves up. *Who knew sex was such a strenuous activity.* A strenuous but amazing activity.

My mind hadn't revived enough for much, so I let myself fall asleep. My chest pressed up against his back, both of us slick with sweat. Both of us still naked.

Chapter Two

I woke up to the sun shining in my face.

I squinted against the light. Became suddenly aware I was not in my own dorm. A movement beside me alerted me to the fact I wasn't alone either. I turned my head. There was a tussled, blond head next to me on the pillow.

The events from last night came back in flashes. *Oh my gad.*

We were still lying atop the covers, our nakedness on display for anyone to see. *Oh gad.* This was obviously someone's room. That someone must've wanted to head to bed sometime in the night. Only we'd occupied it. Lay naked on it. Had sex on it. *Oh no.* Someone must've come in and seen us. Or maybe that someone had pulled someone too and gone to their bed. Maybe. Possibly. *Hopefully.*

Panic boiled in my gut. I threw my feet over the edge of the bed. *What have I done?* I anxiously pulled on my clothes, constantly glancing over my shoulder to make sure I hadn't woken him.

I'd had sex. I'd been drunk—I had been,

hadn't I? I *must've* been. I'd completely let my inhibitions and anxieties go, and I'd had *sex*. My hands were clammy. *No protection.* In porn they always used condoms. Everywhere you turned you were always told to use condoms. My hands shook now. *STDs*. That's what happened without protection. *Bloody STDs!* That's how you contracted *HIV*.

I came inside him. Right after I'd pushed inside. It was so mortifying I didn't have words. Yet... that's how it spread. I could feel itching down there, but I refrained from scratching. Was it because of an STD? Or maybe just dried bodily fluids? That could itch, right? But what if Oliver had HIV? What if *I* had HIV?

"You're leaving?" Oliver's sleep-rough voice came from behind me. It had a desperate edge to it. It was as if he couldn't believe I was leaving, or he didn't want me to leave.

I glanced over my shoulder again, but couldn't meet his gaze, so I turned back to zipping up my jeans. I'd left that particular task for last, to get everything else of me covered first. I didn't answer him. Didn't know what to say.

"Will I see you again?"

He doesn't even recognise me. "Maybe." It was highly likely, considering he was in one of my two courses. Besides, we didn't live in a big town. The students probably made up half the population.

It was his turn to be silent now. What else could I say though? That we shared a class, but I was so invisible to everyone else he didn't even know it? No way. It was, though not quite as much as what we'd just done, mortifying.

My hand were on the doorknob when something inside stopped me from slipping out without another word. I wasn't, generally, a rude person. I didn't like conflict, so I tried to be nice and friendly to people that did speak to me. Unless they were being rude, then I could be just as rude back. He wasn't though.

I turned but still couldn't meet his gaze, so I stared at the nightstand. "Last night—I liked it. Don't think I didn't, because I did. It's just that—" *I don't like you*. I ran a hand through my own tussled hair, though it wasn't as long and unruly as his. I didn't know what kind of excuse to give besides the truth, so I settled on not saying anything. I just shrugged.

"It was good." I saw him sitting up out of the corner of my eye. "I wouldn't mind if it happened again. You were good."

Good? I'd hardly even done anything. He'd done all the work. When it had been my turn I'd come too quick to give much of an impression. My face heated again.

My heart beat rapidly in my chest. My hands were clammy again—and so was the rest of me. *Shit, shit, shit. What have I done?* This wasn't how I'd wanted this to happen. *I didn't want to lose my virginity. I don't like him. Why'd I let him take it?*

Oliver looked sad, lost.

I can't stay. I really couldn't. *I could be infected with some horrible disease.* All because of him. Because I'd given in to his advances. *Shit, shit, shit. No way.*

I couldn't face him anymore. Before he could say anything else, I opened the door and strode out, shutting it softly behind me as I didn't want to alert anyone else to my presence.

I managed to slip out of the house unnoticed.

On Wednesday I arrived to class forty-five minutes before it was supposed to start. As I always did. No one was in the classroom then and I could choose my favourite seat without having to worry about people watching and judging me.

I sat down on the seat closest to the wall and put my bag on the other chair so no one would sit next to me. Literature class wasn't as big as the language class, it wouldn't even be close to full, so there was really no worry about anyone sitting down there at all.

I took my laptop out of my bag, opened it, and plugged my earphones in. Once I typed 'The,' it opened up to the last thing I'd been doing. *Damn it*. I'd been looking up symptoms of STDs the night before.

Saturday and Sunday had been spent mostly in bed, watching telly, losing myself in fictional stories instead of thinking about what had happened in my own life. On Monday and Tuesday I'd still been watching series on the telly, but also reading the material for this week's lectures.

For four days the incessant worry about STDs had been there, at the back of my mind, trying its hardest to come forefront. I'd tried just as hard to keep it in the back, by distracting myself with the telly, series, and films. It had worked so-so. Until last night, when I'd caved and gone online to search.

I shouldn't have done it. Not only were there graphic descriptions of the various STDs, but also *pictures*. They'd been, quite frankly, terrifying.

Someone entered the room and I quickly shut down all tabs on my browser except Fronter. Not that I needed it, I'd already downloaded the lecture notes that had been posted for both Literature and Phonetics.

As the clock ticked on, people trickled in at a slow stream. I hid behind my computer screen, headphones still on, though I still hadn't put on any music. The spectre of having an STD was too big to chase away with music now. I couldn't even concentrate on the notes.

I took my headphones off once the professor arrived, but I couldn't focus on the lecture. *How could I be so stupid? Sex without protection…* I always protected myself. Never for sex as I hadn't had it before, but I didn't do things on impulse. I didn't get close to anyone. I had no *friends*. Because people were cruel and I didn't want to subject myself to that. I didn't think I could take it. Loneliness was so much better.

Literature ended and some people left. More people trickled in for Phonetics. One of them was Oliver. I quickly put my headphones back on and pretended to be immersed in whatever was on my screen. I didn't know where he sat, but he didn't approach me. I was in the back, anyway, in the corner. The only places people could sit were in front of me, or the row of desks next to me.

The lecturer arrived, the room quieted down, and I pulled my headphones off. I chanced a glance around. Oliver was closer to the front of the room, laughing with his mates.

During the lecture he was his obnoxious self, hand shooting into the air, asking questions, giving his point of view on Every Single Thing. Like he knew better than the lecturer. It was infuriating. All I wanted was to learn from people who had this as their professions, who loved it and researched it and constantly updated their knowledge. I didn't want to hear his unimportant additional shit, arguing with the lecturer over the tiniest little things.

I busied myself with my laptop, trying to get my head working. I'd read through the lecture, but I should still listen. There would be extra information not on the handout in Fronter. I couldn't function, however, not with the threat of STDs over me and him in front of the room, being all obnoxious.

The two hour lecture ended after forever. I didn't even realise until people started rising from their desks and leaving. I shut my laptop, took out the headphones, then bent over the other chair to put it all away in my rucksack.

"You should've told me we shared a course."

I jerked, startled, as his voice washed over me. Because obviously it was me he was talking to. I glanced up, to my side. He was standing in front of the desk, looking at me with his head tilted slightly to the side.

"What?" My brows drew together in annoyance and I quickly zipped the rucksack shut.

"You know what." He glanced around covertly, then planted his hands on the desk and leant in closer to me. "We had sex without a condom."

"I *know*." Oh yes, I knew.

"Are you negative?" His tone was so casual, so matter-of-fact.

"Of course I am." Now I glanced around, and even thought the room was empty save for a couple students up front talking to the lecturer, the room was empty. "Are you?"

"I am." He tilted his head the other way. He seemed to be studying me, trying to figure me out. He looked exactly like our dog did when she didn't quite understand. "Still, we had unprotected sex. There's still a chance. We should go get tested. The college health clinic is free."

I frowned. "We?"

"Yes, *we*." He scowled down at me now, not quite as happy-go-lucky as usual. "*We* had unprotected sex, so *we* should take a test. Don't you want to know if you're still negative? Or if you're not?" He gave me an indignant look.

He was right. I knew it. Still… I'd never had sex before so I knew I was clean—but *he* obviously wasn't a stranger to the pleasures people got up to in bed. He could have HIV without knowing it. I had no way of knowing how many he'd been with before me.

"Fine." I gave in. At least the anxiety would ease once I got those test results back.

He turned, took a few steps towards the door. "You got a car here?"

I shook my head. "No." I did have my licence, but no car on my own. As a student I couldn't afford that. I wanted to devote all my time these three years to my studies, so I didn't want to get a part-time job. It would take focus away from what was important right now. "Do you?"

"Nope." He started walking again. I grabbed my rucksack and hurried after. "We'll just have to walk then. Good thing the weather's nice." He cast me a grin over his shoulder.

I scowled. What we were about to do—what we'd done—was serious business. He shouldn't be grinning. He should be afraid, as full of anxiety as me. STDs, and especially HIV, were something to be taken seriously.

But then he wasn't often serious, was he?

Chapter Three

"I can't believe this." I murmured it to myself as we sat in the waiting room. We were the only ones there, *thankfully*, but we still had to wait.

"It's so easy to forget them." He was sitting in the chair next to me. Well, more like sprawled in it. His legs were spread wide, his head tilted back to stare up at the ceiling. It was a normal ceiling. White. Nothing at all fascinating about it that I could see. "The condoms. You get drunk and all inhibitions fly out the window."

"You must be used to this then," I said drily.

"Sorry?" He tilted his head towards me. "What's that supposed to mean?"

"Going at it without condoms. Taking HIV tests." I stared back with a blank expression.

He frowned. "Why would that be something I'm used to?" He actually seemed confused.

"Isn't that what you do?" Did he really not realise what I was on about? "Get drunk and sleep around?" I got annoyed as he only blinked. "So if your little theory is true and condoms are forgone in a drunken heat of passion, then this—

" I gestured at the room at large, "—must be normal for you."

His breath hitched, then his eyes narrowed into another frown. "What have I done to offend you?"

That was easy. "You threw yourself at me. I reckon I'm not all that special, so you must do that to lots of other guys too."

"I don't recall you saying no. In fact, from what I remember—and I've got a good memory—you were *all* willing *all* the time."

"You certainly knew what you were doing." The image of him on the bed, dick hard and fingers in his arse... it was an image I did *not* want to have in my mind. "All bossy and straight-forward. How many else have you bossed around like that, huh? How many else have you let fuck you without lube and a condom? You like the pain, the thrill, is that it?" I didn't know where this word-vomit came from. Nor my rudeness. I hated conflict and this was definitely smack up that territory.

He turned his head away. His teeth flashed as he drew his bottom lip into his mouth. "I'm not a slag. Just because I've slept with some guys doesn't make me that. You have no right to come here and judge me. You don't know me."

That was true. Still, I'd had sex with him. He

had thrown himself at me. He'd started it all and I'd simply gone with it.

"You don't know me either. So *why* throw yourself at me?"

"I didn't *throw* myself." He glared at his lap. "I didn't."

I crossed my arms over my chest, staring the opposite way. "Keep telling yourself that." I would've never chosen to get with a stranger if I was on the pull. Not that I would be, but *if*. I'd want at least some kind of connection. I'd want to know the person was nice and not a total madman.

"I like sex, okay? Excuse me if you've got a problem with it. That's not *my* problem, you know. It's natural, it's good. Everyone does it. It's not like it's this big taboo." He sighed. "I'm not going to apologise for liking it. And I'm not going to sit here and let you call me a slag."

He was free to leave. I wasn't keeping him here.

There was strained silence between us now. *Can't I get in to take that bloody test?* I didn't want to sit here with him anymore. "Why me?" I hadn't meant to blurt it out, but I was curious.

"Hmm?"

Was he daft? "Why did you decide to pull me? Because I was the only one available?"

"Don't jump to conclusions," he snapped. "Anyway, I don't know."

"How can you not *know*?"

He sighed heavily, glancing around as if for help. Maybe he wanted to get in to take the test as much as I did to break this up. "I thought you were handsome, and you seemed a bit lost in that bathroom. I just thought I'd go for it."

I stared at him in wonder. A complete stranger—someone who'd been in his class not just this semester, but last one as well, and whom he'd never once noticed… how could he come here and give compliments to my looks? They weren't that great either. "You're taking the piss."

"I'm not."

He was. He had to be. No one had ever complimented me on my looks before. I did have features from both Mum and Dad, but I mostly looked like Dad. I couldn't exactly say he was a beauty.

The receptionist came over to tell us we could now head into the laboratory for our tests.

Another woman was there, in her middle to late thirties as far as I could tell. She wore glasses and typed on a computer for a moment before she turned to us. "Hello." She smiled and wheeled her chair to face us. "You're both here for STD and HIV tests, correct?"

"Yeah." Oliver nodded.

"All right. Which one of you want to go first?"

Oliver glanced at me, but I pointedly looked away.

"I will." He sat down in the chair next to her and rolled up his sleeve. My gaze zeroed in on the colourful bands he wore. *Way to advertise your sexuality.* "I feel like a druggie about to shoot up," he teased as the strap was secured around his upper arm and tightened. The woman prepared a needle, then pressed her finger down in the crook of his elbow to feel the vein.

"This is not funny." I frowned at him. Drugs… Did he have personal experience with them? Or was he simply trying to lift the mood? If he was, it was a shitty way of doing so.

His lips tightened. "Not everyone can be all serious and gloomy."

My eyes narrowed.

The woman chuckled. "You two make a cute couple." She stuck the needle into Oliver's arm and dark red blood began to pour into the phial.

I grimaced. "Cute?" *Of course that's what I had to react to.* I rolled my eyes at myself and crossed my arms defensively.

"Couple?" He grimaced as well—though that might have been from her changing phials—glancing my way.

"Don't be embarrassed." She removed the second phial of blood, then pressed a lump of cotton wool to where the needle penetrated Oliver's skin, before retracting said needle. She then secured the cotton wool with a piece of tape. "We've had gay couples in here before wanting to be tested before they stop using condoms. We recommend it to straight couples as well."

We were not a couple. Not by a long shot. How could that *not* be obvious? Was this kind of bickering normal between couples?

"Oh, we're not a couple." Oliver said it fast, casting a furtive look at me. "You know what it's like, drunk, passionate, it's easy to forget the condoms…" He trailed off. I didn't know if it was because he caught my glare or because he didn't have anything else to add.

She looked between us. "I see."

I took Oliver's seat in the chair and deftly rolled up my right sleeve. She tightened the strap around my arm, and I could see the blue vein through my pale, thin skin. "Maybe you need some condoms then." She nodded towards a bowl standing close to the door while she prepared a new needle. It was filled with brightly coloured condom packages.

"Hey, thanks!" Oliver grinned and grabbed a handful, completely ignoring my still-present glare. What did he need condoms for? Was he going to go out pulling again, so soon after the last time?

There was a painful prick as the needle stuck into my arm, but it faded right away. I watched as my blood flooded into the phial. It was just as dark red as his had been.

I didn't particularly like needles, but this time it was necessary. I didn't want to worry anymore, didn't want to be cooped up in bed watching series because I was trying not to have an anxiety attack over the fact I'd had unprotected sex. My first time having sex and I'd been so stupid I exposed myself to STDs.

Never again.

"Here." He held out his hand, several condom packets resting in his palm, as we exited the building.

"I don't want them." I didn't even want to look at them, but they were glaringly obvious with their bright colours.

"We need to be prepared," he pressed. "You want Friday night to repeat itself? You want to come over here again for them to draw more of your blood?"

"No." Of course I didn't. "I'm not going to get in that position again. I shouldn't have in the first place."

"Sex is natural." He sounded frustrated. With me, probably. "You can't say you won't get into that position again, because odds are you *will*. So will I. It's just the way it is. And we better be prepared." He waved his handful of condoms in front of my face. "Take them."

I did, but only so he'd stop waving them around for everyone to see. I shoved them in my pockets and bowed my head, not even daring to see if anyone was around to watch this spectacle.

"You shouldn't be so worried about what other people think," he said. "Other people's opinions doesn't matter—unless you want them to. And *that* is debilitating, isn't it?"

"I don't care what people say or mean." But I did. I didn't want to stand out, I didn't want to be someone people talked about behind my back. Someone people laughed at. I had enough paranoid thoughts of that happening without adding to them. "People shouldn't advertise their private lives in public. They should stay private."

He sighed audibly. "It was just a few

condoms. Everyone's got condoms. Get over it."

I couldn't just get over it. It was embarrassing. Humiliating even. Though not as humiliating as our so-called sexual encounter, what with how quickly it had all been over for me.

"Have you taken a test like this before?" I asked, quietly now, the fight going out of me in my mortification.

"I have. Of course I have. It should be done every so often, it depends on how often you change partners. Or if you forget the condoms, obviously." He buried his hands in his pockets as we headed back towards the college. My dorm lay beyond it, though I didn't know where he lived. "I was negative last time I took an HIV test. STD tests too. Nothing funny there."

"So you're negative, and I'm definitely negative. In this case, two negatives does not make a positive."

"How can you be so sure?" He tilted his head back, looking skywards. "Didn't you say you hadn't taken an HIV test before?"

"I did say that, yeah." Dammit. He had to remember my exact words? And now he was inquiring about it. "I've never done it before."

"Yeah, you said so—"

"Not an HIV test," I interrupted, annoyed he

didn't understand, but then I deflated as I muttered the next word. "Sex."

"What?" Now I had his attention.

"Do I have to spell it to you?" I got annoyed all over again, blood boiling. "*Sex*. I've never had it. Done it. With *anyone*."

He stared. Like I was some sort of oddity. "How's that possible?"

"It's perfectly possible." Honestly. "Not everyone have an interest in pulling random blokes."

He grabbed my arm, turned me around so I had no choice but to give him my full focus. "Come on. I think you're handsome. It's not possible that no one else haven't been there before me."

"It is quite possible." I pulled my arm roughly out of his grip. "And excuse me if I don't believe you. This is the second semester we share a class, and you had no idea who I was."

He blinked. Looked away. Looked at his feet.

"Just forget it." I started walking again. We were past the college now and I could see the block of flats ahead. There were three next to each other, but I lived in the first one.

"Hey, come on!" He jogged up to my side again. "You can't hold that against me. It's a big class. I don't sit around and study everyone in it."

I didn't want to speak to him anymore. I wanted to go home, wanted to be on my own, and desperately hope the tests turned out okay.

"Did you know who I was?" This came out hesitant, like he was afraid of the answer.

"Hard not to." Considering he was the one who had comments on *everything*.

"You had Grammar and Lexicology last year too?"

Sure had. "Yep." Four months in the same class last semester, and one month into the new one. Almost half a year in close proximity, that.

I upped my speed. The block of flats were coming closer, I could see the whole of it now, not just the upper floors.

Oliver lagged behind. I glanced over my shoulder to see what he was up to, only to find him standing there with a bit of a lost expression. He ran his hand through his hair repeatedly, and kept glancing the way we'd come, back towards the college.

All of a sudden I felt bad.

What was I supposed to do though? I didn't know him. I didn't even like him. It wasn't my job to cheer him up. Besides, he was the cheery one, not me. He seemed to be smiling all the time, laughing and joking with his mates. Now I was the only one around, though, and I *had* been rude, hadn't I? I didn't like being rude, but then I also didn't like him. Sometimes my dislike won over the fact I needed to be nice to avoid conflict.

Should I say something? Go back to him? But I didn't have something to say and if I walked back, what was I supposed to do? Just stand there besides him in silence?

His gaze fell on me and I quickly turned away. Best to go home. I wasn't fit for being sociable anyway. Not with anyone.

It was better for me, and for him, this way. To part ways. We were too different. It wouldn't work. Not that I wanted anything to work, because he got on my every nerve. Some days I could sit and focus solely on my annoyance with him — at his hand always shooting in the air, of his voice always having to add something or argue something — than on the actual lecture.

Best not to get further involved. It'd been more than enough already. More than I'd ever planned, for sure. I didn't know about him, but he had people falling all over him. He could fend for himself.

I, on the other hand, only had myself.

And it was enough.

Chapter Four

"You have to get out more."

That's what my mother kept telling me. Whenever we were on the phone, she always managed to sneak it in somehow. She'd been happy to know I actually had bought a ticket for Friday night's concert at the student house. Only reason I did, though, was because I really did want to listen to that particular band.

So I went, after several anxious rounds with myself. The place was packed with people though, so I blended into the crowd easily. As invisible as always. I liked it. I even had a drink, but it tasted like shit, so I opted out of the alcohol altogether. It wasn't like I had any interest in it. Suppose it was peer pressure, considering everyone else seemed to have a drink or a beer in their hands.

The concert was good. I enjoyed the music, but could've definitely done without the crowded space, the bad air, and drunk students spilling drinks.

Leaving the place was another chapter in

itself. Bodies pressed against me on every side as we all tried leaving at the same time.

It was a relief to finally come out in the cold, crisp winter air.

I was on the pavement, looking left and right for oncoming cars when I saw an unruly blond head out of the corner of my eye. I turned slowly, and yes indeed, there was Oliver. He was leaning against the wall in jeans that had wet spots on them and just a thin jacket. He seemed completely out of it.

No one bothered with him. Everyone left, in pairs or in groups, all chatting amiably. Some were drunk and had to be supported, but the majority had their senses about them. Yet no one cared about him while he struggled to stay on his feet.

Dammit.

I walked over. "Oliver?"

No reaction.

"Oliver? Come on." I put my hand on his shoulder, shaking him the tiniest bit.

"What." His voice was hoarse and slurred. There was no rising intonation at the end. No question. Just him, slurring, too drunk to make sense. Too drunk to think of proper words, probably.

"You need to go home." He couldn't stay out

like this. He'd end up in a ditch somewhere and no one would bother with him. Dressed the way he was, he'd freeze to death.

"No." He swatted at me, but even as close as I was standing he missed.

I couldn't leave him. He wasn't in any kind of state to get home on his own. Since I didn't know where he lived, that only left one option: I had to take him home with me.

"Come on. I'll help you." I took his arm and draped it over my shoulder. I held his hand so it would stay there, then wrapped my other arm around his waist to keep him upright and somewhat steady.

He groaned as we started walking, and I worried he was about to be sick. He stayed upright though and quieted down. His head lolled on his shoulder, then came to rest against mine. "I'm sorry."

I had no idea what he was apologising for. "Come on." The way up to the college was all uphill. It was tiresome going up alone, never mind when I had to drag him with me.

We managed, somehow, and once I'd locked us into my room I was sweating, in a sour mood, and probably red in the face from the exertion. I deposited Oliver on my bed and took off his shoes and jacket so he'd be more comfortable.

After throwing them over my chair, I hovered, not knowing what to do next.

My bed was small. It was a single. Or a little wider than a single, but I used up the space when I slept. How was I going to get any sleep with him in there?

"Oliver?"

He grunted.

"I'm going to take a shower. Do you need anything? Water, painkillers, something to eat?"

Another grunt. He turned over on his side, back to me.

Okay then.

I got more comfortable clothes from my closet and had my shower in the bathroom next door. I felt a lot more refreshed afterward, and my red face had subsided somewhat. I stared at myself in the mirror, dragging my hand over my face as I did so. I had stubble. Not a lot, but enough to be noticeable. I had acne on my forehead, especially my temples, that never seemed to go away no matter what I did. There were some at the back of my neck too.

"It doesn't even matter," I muttered to myself, pulling my clothes on.

I got a glass of water for Oliver, and took the bucket we used for washing the floors as a safety measure. It wasn't like anyone was going to use it during the night, after all.

He was still on his side when I got back in my room. His breathing had evened out, so he was fast asleep. He was also still in his wet jeans.

I sighed, but I had to do something. He was atop the duvet too.

The jeans were first. I unzipped them, my mind flashing back to last Friday and how he'd unbuttoned them wantonly himself then. There was nothing erotic about our current predicament though, so those thoughts should stay far away.

I got them off eventually. He'd woken enough to grunt at me, but fell asleep again as I pulled them off his legs. He was only in a pair of tight boxer briefs now. During my struggle getting his jeans off, he'd turned onto his back. My gaze was drawn to those white briefs and what hid underneath. There was a bump there, outlining his… appendage.

I shouldn't be ogling him, but I couldn't help it. I'd seen him naked. I'd done a lot more than see him naked. We'd had sex. It had been good. *He'd* been good. Good with his mouth, and good to be inside—for the short time I had been, anyway.

"I'm sorry." It came out a whisper. I'd been so rude to him two days before. Now he was in my bed, pissed and helpless. I didn't even want to think about what could've happened if I hadn't seen him, if I hadn't brought him here with me.

Maybe he was obnoxious. Maybe he always had to have a say in anything—but he hadn't actually been unpleasant to me. He'd made the first move on me, he'd approached me after class worried about us contracting STDs because we hadn't used condoms. He'd offered to go take the tests together. And when I'd left him at the pavement, halfway home, he'd seemed so lost. I couldn't get that image out of my mind.

I suppose he was kind of… good-looking. When he kept his mouth shut.

A yawn escaped me. I was tired. I only had my bed. No extra mattress, no extra sheets. We had to share the bed, there was no other way about it. I wasn't about to sleep on the floor, or in my uncomfortable chair.

"Oliver?"

Nothing.

"Scoot over."

Still nothing.

I pushed on his shoulder.

He groaned. But he did do as I wanted and turn on his side again. I pushed him further in, almost up against the wall.

I slipped into bed, with my back to his, and pulled the duvet over us. It was cold, but it'd warm up quick. Maybe even quicker when we were two sharing body-heat?

He was warm against my back. I, on the other hand, was freezing. Even if I was in joggers and a tee. It was normal though, I was always cold when the temperature in the room dropped. I should turn the heater up, but now that I was in bed and under the duvet I couldn't be bothered to get up and do it.

My eyelids were heavy. I was very much aware of his back against mine, of his even breathing. The bucket was at the end of the bed—and I realised I should've pushed him further towards the edge of the bed so I could slip in on his other side.

It was too late now, though.

My bedtime was past a while ago. I always went to bed early, and got up early. I felt I got more out of the day that way, instead of staying up half the night and sleeping half the day away.

I let my eyelids fall shut.

What was I going to do in the morning? When he was sober and awake with me, probably wondering why I'd brought him home with me when I'd so explicitly made myself clear I didn't want to have anything to do with him.

Except maybe I did. But no. He really *was* obnoxious. I'd be constantly annoyed if I did have something to do with him. That wasn't ground for friendship. Or a relationship. I shouldn't go there though. No way. I'd never wanted that. I wasn't ready for it. I had enough with myself and my, sometimes, debilitating anxiety.

The thought of the next morning brought that anxiety forefront. It didn't last long, however, because I slowly fell asleep. I was too tired to fight it—besides, why would I?

Morning stiffy.

That's what I woke up to. Both mine and his. Mine was only noticeable to me, but his was pressed against my bum. His arm was around my waist, his head resting against the back of mine. He was a *furnace*.

I kicked the duvet off. He didn't even stir.

I managed to get out from under his arm, and I, as quietly as I could manage, headed into the bathroom.

There I leaned against the sink and stared at myself in the mirror, just like I'd done last night. My hair looked a bit wonky, since I'd gone to bed with it wet, but it was short enough for that to be rectified with a little bit of water.

My joggers were tented.

What was I supposed to do about that? I'd never wanked off before. I'd touched it before, when I'd woken up to it like this, but never actually got off. I always waited it out. But I had to go in there again, and I couldn't look like this. Could I?

He would still look like this. I hoped, at least, so I wouldn't be the only one. Now that would definitely be mortifying.

I brushed my teeth, thoughts churning. What if he was awake? What was I supposed to say and do? What if he was still asleep? What *then*? Should I slip into bed with him again?

I pulled my T-shirt down as I left the bathroom, but it only covered the hem of my joggers. I tried to press down on the source of my problem, but it didn't seem to want to subside. It was stiff. There was no hiding it. My joggers weren't *that* baggy.

He *was* still asleep.

I locked the door, then stood there uncertain. I didn't have many choices. I could slip back in bed, but what would be the point? I was awake. I wasn't going to be able to sleep again until tonight. I could sit in the chair, but it was uncomfortable. That's why it always held clothes I hadn't bothered folding and putting in the closet. I could sit at my desk, but wouldn't typing on the keyboard be a little loud in the quiet room? I definitely couldn't put on the telly.

I took a step forward so I could see the entirety of my bed. The bookcase stood before it, because I'd tried to separate bed from office space. *Quite an office.* Just the bookcase, a desk, and a chair. But it was enough. It wasn't like I had space for anything else.

He was on his back again. When I'd kicked the duvet off, I'd left him lying exposed too. He was still in his jumper—and his legs were still bare. His briefs contained one stiff cock lying to the side. They were too tight for it to point upwards, though I was sure it would if those briefs were to come off.

Dammit. I turned away, telling myself off for thinking like that, only to crash into my chair. It almost tipped over, and so did I with it, but I managed to keep both of us upright. "Ow. Bloody—" My toes hurt like hell, they had hit the chair's leg full-force.

There was a sharp intake from the bed and it creaked.

Oh shit. My face must be bright red again. I could feel it growing hot. I turned slowly, and yes, he was now awake because I was incapable of moving around my own room.

Chapter Five

Oliver rubbed his eyes, then stared at me. "Adrian." He blinked, looked around, then blinked some more at me. "Umm—"

"You were drunk." I hurried to explain. "You couldn't stand on your feet or talk to me. So I—I didn't have a choice. I had to bring you here."

His gaze fell down my body. I knew exactly which body part had drawn his attention. Now I wasn't busy avoiding his eyes, my gaze was drawn a certain somewhere too.

"That was nice of you." His tongue peaked out to lick his lips. "Ugh." He grimaced. "My mouth still tastes like beer."

That must be a horrible taste. "I've got an extra toothbrush, if you want." I had bought it for myself, I just hadn't got around to open the package yet. Good thing now, though.

He nodded. He was still staring at my groin. I couldn't exactly say anything, because I was still staring at his.

"Bathroom's out here." I motioned towards the door. "Door on the left right outside."

"Yeah, okay." He threw his feet over the edge of the bed and when he stood I could see him even clearer. Well, a certain part of him. Through white boxer briefs.

I turned away quickly and led the way into the bathroom. The packet was in my shelf. The cabinet wasn't big, only three shelves, and my neighbour had a lot more stuff than I did, so he had two of them. "Here."

"Thanks."

I handed him my toothpaste too. He did quick work of it. "This is amazing," he muttered around the toothbrush, brushing in quick, hard strokes.

Strokes… Okay, I needed to get my head out of the gutter. "You want a shower too?"

"Can I? Thanks!" He grinned down, then took the toothbrush out and spit into the sink. He put it under the water, then stuck it in his mouth again.

That mouth had been around me last week.

"I'll get you a towel." It was only five steps or so from the bathroom to the furthest closet. I only had a couple towels, and I got the biggest, fluffiest one. "Here."

He was done brushing his teeth when I came back in. Now he turned to me, flashing those briefs and what was straining inside them again.

I was like a moth to a light; I *couldn't* look away.

"You want to take a shower *with* me?"

I took a startled step back and lifted my head. His eyes were narrowed slightly, studying me, and there was a small grin on his lips. *He knows*. He knew I wanted him. I did, no matter how much my head said I didn't, my other head knew otherwise.

"Come on, Adrian." He took a step closer.

I took another back, which resulted in stumbling down from the threshold. "I took a shower last night." Now I really couldn't look at him.

"If you're sure." He leaned against the door now.

My face burned. "I am." I turned into my room. He closed and locked the bathroom door, and only then did I close mine. "Damn." I leaned my forehead against it. My... cock—why couldn't I say it without an embarrassed pause yet?—still stood at proud attention, still tenting my joggers. No wonder he offered to share a shower. The bloody morning stiffy wasn't going *down*. It was all because of him, because I couldn't stop thinking about last Friday night.

The shower started, and I went to sit on the bed. I listened to the water and I couldn't help imagine how it looked like beating down over him. He was naked in there now, as naked as I'd seen him only a week ago. As naked as I wanted to see him *again*. "Shit."

I pressed down on my groin. It was still as engorged as when I'd woken up. As the water was still running, I took a quick peek under the hem of my joggers. Maybe I should start wearing briefs too, or at least my tight boxers. The loose ones didn't hide a thing.

After a quick round with myself, I also pulled the hem of the boxers up so I could peek at myself in full, naked glory.

To think I'd never once given thought to sex before, but now I'd had it I couldn't stop imagining it. Our actions last Friday… they ran on repeat in my head. The way he'd been sprawled on the bed, fingers inside, cock erect. How his mouth had sucked me and then how his body had sucked me *in*.

I liked it. No doubt about it. A glistening tear of pre-come appeared at the head of my dick, slowly sliding down until it came to rest in my pubes. Which looked a wild bush no one had ever trimmed. I should've shaved in the shower last night. Should've done something.

But how could I have known I'd wake up like this? That he'd wake up like he had? Blokes didn't wake up with morning stiffs every day, did they? I certainly didn't. Did he?

The door handle pushed down and I quickly let go of them hem of both boxers and joggers as I sat up straight.

Oliver came inside, jumper and tee in hand, and with just the towel wrapped around his hips. His chest, his smooth chest, was on display for me to ogle.

He came closer, to stand in front of me. One of his hands clutched something and when he held it out towards me I saw it was my box of Vaseline.

"It was the only slick I could find."

Slick?

The towel fell to the floor. I was on eye-level with one hard cock.

"Where do you have the condoms?"

I licked my lips. They'd suddenly gone dry. As had my mouth.

"Adrian? The condoms?"

I tilted my head to the side. "In the bottom drawer."

He followed my line of sight to the desk. He took the two—three steps over to it and bent over to get said condoms. I'm sure he did it on purpose, giving me one glorious view, because he honestly didn't have to bend over *that* much just to get to the drawer.

I was frozen in place on the bed. I had no idea what to do. What did he expect me to do? Get naked, maybe. I couldn't get my body to move, though.

He came back, threw both Vaseline and a condom packet on the bed besides me, then bent down. His fingers grabbed the hem of my joggers and boxers, just like I'd done not long ago, and he slowly pulled them down. The only thing I managed was to lift my bum a bit so he *could* get them off of me.

A breathy sound left him, like a laugh, except… not. His hand wrapped around me, stroking softly. My breath hitched.

"We'll be good today." He took the condom packet and ripped it off with his teeth. I would not have managed it as gracefully as he did, but then he had a lot of practice, whereas I had none. "Haven't got our test results back yet, so better not tempt fate." He rolled the condom on me oh-so-slowly.

I'd never worn a condom before. It looked weird, too tight, and a bit stupid with the extra space on the end. It was like it didn't fit, yet it did. I'd seen it in porn, I knew it was supposed to be like this, that the semen had to get space in there too once it got that far.

He leaned in closer, tongue coming out to

lick just underneath the head of my dick. "Good, right?"

I could only nod. Of course it was good. I wouldn't be sitting here with a stiffy, letting him put a condom on me, if it wasn't.

He went down on me, throat muscles tightening around me. *Deep-throating. Bloody hell.*

His hair was right there, the only thing in my line of sight right now as he worked me. I lifted one hand and tangled my fingers in the wet, ruffled lengths. Not that it was long, per se, but enough to grab a good hold of.

His mouth around me felt just as amazing as it had the first time around. Too amazing. I was going to embarrass myself again.

"Oliver." I pushed at his shoulders. He didn't move, he didn't *get* it. I pushed harder. "Oliver. Stop."

That word did it. He pulled back, wiped some spit from the corners of his mouth. "What? Didn't you like it?"

"I—I did." How could I make him understand without making myself sound completely ridiculous? "I just…"

A grin spread slowly on his face. "You want to get to the main event, don't you?"

It hadn't been that exactly, but I grabbed hold of the excuse, nodding to show him he was right.

"Right then. You lie down." Now he pushed me, palms against my chest. "No, wait."

I caught myself with my arms before falling onto my back. "What?" Had he changed his mind?

"Your shirt." He crawled onto the edge of the bed, his thighs sliding under mine. "Get it off." It was a request I do it, but he was the one who slipped his hands under it and bunched it up under my arms. "Lift up."

I did and he got the T-shirt off, throwing it haphazardly away before he descended on me. Now I let myself fall back, just barely managing to beat my head against the wall.

He landed atop me, lips on mine ready for a kiss, but he was laughing instead.

I hit his shoulder playfully, but felt embarrassed at the near miss. Why did I always have to be so awkward in social situation? Apparently I was just as awkward in sexual situation too. Weren't they supposed to be easy? They always were on telly or in books. Real life, not so much.

"You shouldn't be so serious, Adrian. Lighten up a bit. Let loose."

Easy for him to say, who was so easy-going and social and well-liked. Except by me, but I was warming up to him. More than warming up—certain parts of me *were* up and wanted attention.

"Adrian. Come on." His tongue licked over my lips. "It was funny, okay? Sex is fun. Whatever awkwardness happens during sex is fun. Just laugh it off. I do."

I couldn't. But he didn't seem to mind, so the least I could do was try to put it behind me and live in the moment. Also a hard thing to do. I always worried.

He kissed me proper now, tongue and all in my mouth. That was more like it.

Our cocks rubbed together, his bare, mine still had the condom on. It didn't take away any of the pleasure, that was for sure.

Kissing was good too, though a bit sloppy. Suppose that was what it was like though when tongues were involved. I couldn't complain. He felt so damn *good*.

"Going to rock your world tonight, babe." He grinned against my lips, then sat up, stretching his arms over his head.

A strangled laugh left me. "I can't believe you just said that."

He grinned, unrepentant. His blond hair was as unruly as ever and it was starting to dry by now. He looked glorious like that, stretching his lean body, sitting atop me, about to get *on* me.

He grabbed the Vaseline, threw the top cap off and stuck three fingers down in the gooey mass. I watched those fingers until they disappeared behind him. His eyelids closed, hand moving, hips rocking.

"Stroke yourself. Keep it ready."

He was so crude, so vocal. It should bother me, like it did in class, but now I found it hot. So I did as he said, wrapping my fingers around myself. I hadn't done this before, either. It was awkward. His eyes were still closed, so it didn't matter, I kept on it.

"Ahhh, yeah." His fingers came out, he grabbed more Vaseline, but this time they slathered me up.

I watched, tense—because I didn't want it to be over as quickly as it had been last time—but also excited, because *sex*.

He scooted forward. He held onto my cock as he positioned himself, then he slowly sank down. His body let me in, and the warmth and the tightness were almost my undoing. *Again*.

Someone moaned. Him or me, it was a toss-up. Maybe both of us. He started out slow, sliding up and down in an almost languid fashion, but he gradually increased until the most audible thing in the room, besides moans, was our skin slapping.

I grabbed onto his thighs, trying to hold myself together, to last just a little bit longer. I didn't manage. My body tensed, my fingers clamped on his thighs, and the orgasm rocked through me.

Time seemed to disappear for a moment. It was just me, him, and the incredible rush an orgasm brought.

He rose enough to let my cock slip out of him, then he sat back down and stroked himself in a hurried frenzy. "Almost there. *Almost.*" I was mesmerised by the way he worked himself. Of how his whole head glistened as he stroked down, and how the foreskin bunched up and covered it when he stroked up.

"Ahh, yeah, *there.*" White spurts erupted from his slit, landing on my stomach, some trickling down his cock to land in my pubes. It was warm and sticky.

Once he started to soften, he leaned down to give me a sloppy kiss. Only lips on lips this time, no tongue in the mix. "*That* was amazing." He fell onto his side next to me, in the little space there was between me and the wall.

"You don't think it ended a bit—well, quickly?" My face was flushed again, embarrassed by yet being unable to last for any amount of time.

"Premature ejaculation happens to everyone." He slid his arm over my chest, fingers tweaking a nipple as he did so. "Especially if this is only your second time. Don't worry, I'm not holding it against you." He moved around, finding a comfortable position, then he put his head on my shoulder. "You should've seen me my first times. Not much to brag about, I can tell you that. They didn't come back for seconds, so they must've thought so too." He yawned. "Almost no one ever comes back for seconds."

His finger circled my nipple now.

No seconds. What did that mean? That he did sleep around a lot, or that those he actually wanted to sleep with only were with him one night for the sex and then didn't bother the next day?

That sounded an awful lot like me last Saturday. "I'm sorry about last weekend. I was an arsehole."

"Yep. You were." He moved on to my other nipple, circling it, lightly tweaking, teasing. "But it's okay, because here we are."

Here we were, indeed. What it did mean though? I was afraid to ask. Since I'd been back for seconds, did it mean I would be getting a third helping too? Did it mean he wanted me to?

I could drive myself mad speculating. I wasn't brave enough to ask either.

"Are you an English major?" That was a safer topic. "I mean, you aren't in the Literature class. You weren't last semester either, so…"

"Nah. I'm majoring in Drama and Theatre. I'm just taking the English language course to improve my English. Need that if I want to go international."

Drama and theatre. *Figures*. No wonder he was so out there. He was one of those kinds, who wanted to live off of that, of playing someone else, of being on stage. He was loose, care-free, not at all afraid to put himself out there. What was he doing here with me? I was wrapped in a blanket of anxiety, all the time. It was exhausting, but it was also safe.

"So you're an English major then?"

"Yeah."

"What do you want to do with your education once you're done? You got any plans?"

"Don't know, really." I had an idea. "I'm thinking about working in publishing. I like books. I'm good at language. Editor, maybe." An office job where I got to do what I liked. I had to converse with people, but it was different than working at the supermarket, for example, where you had to be all welcoming and smiling all the time. It wasn't me.

"That sounds interesting. I could never do it, though." He feigned a shudder. "Sitting at a desk all day— I wouldn't have the patience for it. I need to be up and moving, living life."

We were so different. It was impossible for this to work out. If there was anything to work out to begin with. I didn't know—and I didn't ask.

I was afraid of the answer.

I didn't know which answer I was afraid of, though.

And *that* made my anxiety worse.

Chapter Six

"I think we both need a new shower."

We'd been silent for so long I'd started to dose off. "Hmm?"

"Shower. You and I. Together." He sat up, leaning on one arm. "Come on. It's hot. And I don't just mean the water." He climbed atop me, bum brushing my flaccid cock, then he climbed over me to stand on the floor.

He lifted the towel he'd discarded and threw it over his shoulder. "I can use this one again." He looked around some more. "Where's my jeans?"

"They were wet. Smelled of beer." I'd folded them and put them next to the bag that held my dirty laundry. "You can borrow something from me though."

"Great!" A wide smile.

Was that all it took? To be nice to him? Was that all he needed to be happy and smiling? Sure seemed like it.

"Come on." He motioned to me and I groaned as I got out of bed. I'd been so comfortable, I hadn't wanted to leave it. But he was right, a shower was needed. I was full of semen. And — I stared down at myself. I still had the condom on.

He saw it now too, and he started laughing. He came over, hands dropping to cup my balls. "Want me to take it off for you?" He leaned in, nipped at my jaw, lips sliding up to hover next to mine. He didn't wait for my reply, but got the condom off without any hassle. He stepped back, tied it, threw it in the rubbish, and then he boldly opened the door to head into the bathroom.

"Jesus," I muttered. What if my neighbour had been out there? He wasn't, thankfully, but he *could've* been.

I grabbed my joggers and T-shirt and hurried after him, locking the bathroom door once I was inside. "You're mad."

"How so?" He was still smiling as he hung the towel up over the one I'd used last night.

"I've got a neighbour. We share this bathroom. What if he'd been in the hallway?"

"It's just a bit of nakedness, Adrian. Chill." He pressed close to me. Certain… spent… body parts pressed together. "When we were younger we always had to get naked in the showers after gym. Everyone knew what their classmates looked like in the nude. It's no big deal. All natural."

For him, maybe. He seemed comfortable with himself. I wasn't.

He turned away from me to turn the shower on, but he bent over to do so, he pushed his bum out, right up to my groin. I drew in a sharp breath.

"Feels good, doesn't it?" He wriggled his bum.

My nether regions liked it. They tingled as blood rushed south, slowly — oh, so slowly — hardening up again.

"Y-yeah." I wanted to thrust forward, right into his tight heat, but managed to restrain myself. He might still be slathered with Vaseline, but I was bare. No condom. The rest of them were still in the bottom-most drawer in my desk.

He straightened up again and lifted his arm up and behind my neck, pulling me in close. Now we touched from groin and up. Well, from bum and up, in any case. He moved against me, rubbing against me almost. My cock fit snugly in-between his arse-cheeks and he made the most of that, moving his hips up and down.

"You too." He held fast at my neck so my head rested against the side of his. I did start moving my own hips, thrusting forwards and up, then back and down. It wasn't as good and as tight as being inside him, but I wasn't complaining. This was something new too. I'd done a lot of new things in the last week. I never would've imagined it before.

As we moved against each other, he somehow found the wits to turn the shower on. A few cold drops splattered on me, but it quickly turned warm. He stepped forward and I followed, didn't want to be parted from him now we had something so good going. The water washed down over us as we kept our rhythm.

"Yeah. *Yeah*. *Oh* so good." That was him. I didn't think I'd be comfortable being that vocal. Not yet. Maybe not ever. It required a lot more guts than I had. I couldn't even speak up in class, not even when I was certain of the answer. It was too terrifying.

I was getting close to another orgasm. It was evidenced by the sudden jerky motions of my hips.

"No, no, no. Don't come yet." He turned around quickly, his erect cock bumping hello against mine. "I want to suck you. Suck that orgasm out of you. I want to *taste* you."

Now that sounded lewd. And *so* hot.

He positioned me against the wall before

sinking to his knees. He let his lips slide over me first, then he licked one long path up the underside of my cock. He stared up at me as he did, our gazes meeting. When he took me fully into his mouth our gazes still held.

I watched, completely mesmerised, as his cheeks hollowed when he sucked. His lips were tight and snug around me, sliding further down, back up, down again... I could never get enough of watching him do this. I could never get enough of how it felt to have it done.

How I'd managed to go so many years without it was beyond me. The age of consent was sixteen, and statistically I believed lads lost their virginity either before or right after that point. Maybe their statistics were seventeen? I might've read that somewhere. Still, I was six years behind. I was three years into my twenties and only now had I discovered one of the greatest pleasures of all. It was tragic, really.

I needed to grab onto something. The only thing nearby I could grab was him, so I did. I held his head between my hands as he sucked and I came. My hips jerked forward of their own accord, driving me further into his mouth. I could *feel* him swallow what spurted out of me.

"Bloody hell." I was boneless, dried out. I couldn't take any more of this, not today. Two orgasm was enough. Two quick ones, but they were still all-consuming when they happened. I couldn't keep my legs under me, so I slid to the floor.

He laughed at me again. "You taste so good, Adrian." He wiped at the corner of his mouth, where a white drop remained. "Your turn now, all right?" He stood, his cock still full and hard. He straddled my thighs, then bent his knees until the tip of his cock was against my lip.

Oh shit. He wanted me to do what he'd done. I couldn't do that. I'd never done it before, I wouldn't even have a clue what to do.

"Adrian." His cock-head bumped my lips, begging to be let in.

I couldn't tell him no. I couldn't tell him I couldn't do this. So I opened my mouth and though he pushed the head inside, he didn't push further. If he had, I might've gagged. As it was, the head was more than enough.

He was so good at sucking, and his mouth had been moist with spit. Mine was dry. Completely dry. How was I supposed to manage this when there was almost no spit to speak of?

"Yeah, come on." He pushed himself a little further in. "You can do it. I know you can."

I couldn't look up at him. Not like he'd done to me earlier. All I saw was his groin, skin and pubes, and the rest of the length waiting to be let inside. *I can't take all of that.* I couldn't.

I sucked experimentally. The plump head was soft. It had a few drops of salty pre-come on it too. My tongue pressed up, tip licking just underneath the ridge.

He moaned, which meant I must be doing something right.

It wasn't bad having a cock in my mouth. Besides the fact the saliva still seemed to be missing, the silky feel of it was *good*. The head was the best part. I pulled back a bit so I only had to suck on that, not more of his length. I wrapped my hand around the rest, mostly so he wouldn't push it further in, but also because I needed to do something with that hand. The other had clamped around the back of his thigh.

"Yes, Adrian." He gasped. "Suck me, just like that. And stroke. Yes, stroke me."

So that was what I was supposed to do. I did it, though just as awkwardly as I'd been stroking myself earlier. I was getting the hang of sucking though. Saliva was making its return too, maybe by help of the pre-come that kept leaking out his slit.

I closed my eyes, tried to put my own anxieties behind me and just let this happen. Let myself live in the here and now, do what needed to be done in the here and now. Suck him like a pro, though maybe not. I sucked, but I didn't fool myself there was any kind of skill behind it. There couldn't be, being unskilled in everything pertaining to sex. But with practice…

"Ahhh!" The shout alerted me a split second before he came, thick, creamy come spurting into my mouth. A complete surprise. I pulled back, gagging and spitting it onto the wet tiles. More landed on my shoulder as I leaned over, and now I heard Oliver wank himself off until completion.

I watched it out of the corner of my eye, humiliated again by my own actions. He'd swallowed everything I had to give. Why couldn't I extend the same courtesy?

He groaned now as he emptied himself, then he dropped down across my thighs and caught my mouth in a deep kiss. My mouth still had semen in it. He lapped it up. His *own* semen. It tasted—I couldn't quite describe the taste. A bit bitter, salty maybe? Unfamiliar, anyway.

"Mmm." He nuzzled against me, kissing me deeply again, before leaning in for a hug. He seemed satisfied, happy. I should be too, but I couldn't stop obsessing over my own failures.

The water beat down over his back and our legs. The air was steamy, the room hot. I wasn't sure if the hot water ever ran out in the block, as I wasn't in the habit of long showers, but I didn't want to find out either. Showering in cold water would *not* be a good experience.

"We need to finish," I said, hands running slowly down his back. "Wash up."

"Yeah." He only hugged tighter though. "Yeah, okay." He let me go and stood up, hand extending down to me. I took it as I used the other to heave myself up. He pulled and I stumbled in so we were pressed together again. "Please don't change your mind again." He seemed insecure now, eyes big and begging. He seemed so *young*.

Speaking if which, how old was he?

"I—I won't." I wasn't sure that was a promise I could make though. I liked us together like this, alone and intimate, but once we were back in the same class and he was back to being obnoxious again... I might change my mind then. He'd always been a source of annoyance to me, ever since the first day of our language course last year.

A smile. That bloody wide, happy smile. "Good." He bumped our noses together. Good thing I didn't see it coming, or else I might've moved too so we'd butted heads instead.

We finished up in the shower, taking turns

under the water. Once the water was shut off, I hurried to throw his towel at him and wrap mine around me. I felt incredibly self-conscious now the sex was over. I wanted to get dressed, to get those protective layers around me.

"You're a bit uptight." He watched me in the mirror as I struggled into my clothes. I should've dried off better, that way they wouldn't be sticking to me now. He, on the other hand, stood there naked and proud of it.

I didn't deign that with an answer. "I'll go get some clothes for you."

I was so busy getting out of there I didn't stop to listen. And just like I'd been afraid of earlier, when we'd headed for the shower, I came face to face with my neighbour. He was locking his door, all dressed up for the cold weather outside.

"Hey, Adrian." He had a look on his face. I couldn't quite read it. Teasing, maybe? "Heard you've been having a good morning."

Heard? My face flushed instantly.

He chuckled. "I guess you haven't noticed? The walls between our two rooms might be thick and good at keeping sound out, but the *doors*. Not so much."

Oh shit.

"Don't sweat it, mate." He clapped me on the

shoulder as he brushed past to get to the door. "It's not like I haven't heard it before. Or *done* it before."

I stood there, hoping the ground would open and swallow me whole. I hadn't even thought about what he'd *hear*.

"And the beds?" He turned once he was out in the other hallway, leaning on the other. "They *creak*."

If I didn't burst into flames right about now—

"Come on, man. Light up. It's all good fun." He sounded like Oliver. Speaking of which, he was conspicuously silent.

"Right." It came out in a low mumble.

He chuckled again. "I'm surprised you haven't heard us, to be honest. Or have you?"

"Us?"

"Yeah. My girlfriend and I."

Oh. "No. I haven't."

"Maybe you will." One of his eyebrows quirked good-naturedly. "Have fun, Adrian." He reached in to clap me on the shoulder again, then closed the door.

I dragged my hands over my face.

Muffled laughter could be heard from behind me.

"Shut up, Oliver." I took a pair of tight boxer-briefs, joggers, and a T-shirt from my closet. Once I was in the bathroom, I held them out to him. "Here."

He turned, body on full display. He was shaking from all the laughter he was keeping in.

"What?" I didn't like being laughed at.

"S-sorry," he hiccupped. "It's just—that was *so* funny."

"It really wasn't." It was mortifying. Like everything that happened in my life lately.

"Chill out, Adrian." Still laughing, still naked, still shaking. His flaccid cock drew my focus, though I tried to look everywhere else but at it. "Don't you know what fun is?"

"Not with people." That slipped out. I hadn't meant to say it. It was true, but he didn't have to know just how asocial I was.

He frowned. "What's that mean?"

"That I like being in my own company." I held the clothes out again but he didn't seem to have any interest in them whatsoever.

"So you don't like to be around people?" He eyed me side-ways, confused and trying to make sense of me.

"No."

"But why not?" He threw his arms out. "Don't you get lonely?"

"Not really, no." I had bad days where I

wished I had friends, someone to be close to, but those days were rare. Usually I liked being by myself, liked not having to deal with other people's bullshit. Liked to not have anxiety over every little word I spoke.

"You, Adrian, are weird." I would've been offended if he hadn't stepped up to me and cupped my bum in his palms just then. "So weird." He pressed our groins together, squeezed my cheeks tighter. "And so fucking sexy."

Now that was taking it too far.

"Do you think I am?" he prodded, pressing his groin harder against mine.

When he was all naked, he definitely was. "Sure." When he was dressed and sitting in class… not so much. Then he annoyed me. How could it be possible to be annoyed by someone as much as I was, yet still so turned on when he was naked and willing in private?

"You're such a sweet-talker," he teased, leaning in to nip at my neck. "And by that I mean you're not. At all."

"I got that much, thank you."

The nipping turned into sucking. *I hope he's not planning on making a hickey*. I didn't much fancy walking around with one visible on my neck.

I didn't know what to do with my hands. They hung limply at my sides, but he was squeezing my arse with his and his mouth was attached to my neck. I felt I should be doing something too.

I put them on his waist. His skin was soft and warm, and still a bit damp from the shower. I wanted to feel more, so I moved them down, over his hips, the curve of his bum, down the upper part of his thighs… I knew what I really wanted to do. But did I dare do it?

He was still sucking on my skin, moving slowly down my neck.

I'm doing it. I went for his cock. It was soft now it was flaccid, hanging there with his balls. I ran my fingers over them too, feeling the wrinkled skin, the size and shape of them.

A door opened, and I didn't realise it was the one into our hallway, before my neighbour suddenly appeared, key ready to unlock his own door.

I pushed Oliver away, and shoved my clothes against his chest. He took them automatically. I could tell he was taken aback by my sudden move.

"Sorry, man!" Pål turned to wave at me. "Just forgot something—" He'd caught sight of Oliver and now stood there holding his key aloft for a split second before he realised what he was doing and quickly turned back to his door.

How mortifying could this day become?

Oliver only managed to slip into the boxer briefs before Pål came back out of his room. I could tell he didn't want to look but that he couldn't help but do it anyway.

"Hey, man." Oliver waved cheerfully.

He nodded, then threw his hand up in another wave. "Have fun!"

This time when he closed the door after him, I hurried out to lock it. Then I leant against it as I pressed my hands to my face, anxiety coursing through me. What must he have thought of me, standing in the bathroom we shared with a naked bloke? He'd heard us have *sex*.

"Hey." Oliver's voice washed over me. "Weren't you out to him?"

Out to him? "I'm not out to anyone. There wasn't ever anything to be out about." Since I'd never had any interest in other people, the only label added to me was asocial. I'd never thought in lines of sexuality. I hadn't had need of one. Not until now.

He was silent. I didn't dare look at him to try and determine why. What did *he* think of me, of what I'd just told him? Did he think I was pathetic for never having had any sort of human interaction with anyone besides family?

"Do you want to go for pizza? I'm starving."

Now there was a complete turn of conversation. My anxiety subdued until it slowly faded into the constant little niggle that was always left behind, no matter how calm and secure I was.

"Y-yeah." I was starving too, come to think of it. "Sounds good."

It did mean I had to spend time with him outside my little dorm room though. Would he go back to annoying me, like he did in class? Or was that annoyance only reserved for classes?

I couldn't start worrying myself up about that though.

I'd find out soon enough.

Chapter Seven

"We could take the pizza with us back to your room?" He bumped his shoulder with mine playfully. "If you want."

"I'm okay staying here." I could see the sign of the Pizzeria now. I wasn't sure I was being completely honest, but going back to my room would mean more sex. I could tell from the tone of his voice. And while it was good… I'd had my fill for the day.

"If you're sure."

"I am."

Was he disappointed? I couldn't tell.

We headed inside, was shown to a table, given menus, and asked if we wanted to order drinks. I only wanted water, Oliver: a Cola.

"So what kind of pizza do you like?" He opened the menu and held it out in front of him, almost hiding his entire head from view.

"Just regular ones. Margarita or pepperoni. Or perhaps the one with ham and beef." I was a picky eater. So not only was I anxiety-riddled with everything else, I also had to watch what kind of food I was served. Mushrooms in particular were vile—and I couldn't force them down my throat if I tried.

"Don't like anything fancy on it, huh?"

Was that said in a teasing tone? What was there to tease about? "No. Plain and simple is fine with me."

He lowered his menu so he could look across at me. "Good thing I'm plain and simple then."

It took me a second—but then my face flushed in embarrassment. "We're out in public," I hissed.

"Oh, come on!" He glanced around the room. "I bet two thirds of the people in here are couples."

"So?" I did a covert glance around as well. "At least they keep it on the down low. It's private. It should be kept *private*."

He rolled his eyes. "So you're one of those guys."

"What guys?" Why was it so difficult for him to understand that I wasn't comfortable talking about such private things in public? Did he go and regularly discuss such things aloud?

"The guys you can't even hold hands with, because they're either still half-way in the closet or too embarrassed to be seen with someone who *is* out and proud—who everyone else *knows* is out and proud." He put his menu down flat, hands smoothing over it in jerky motions.

"I'm not in any closet. But yeah, I get easily embarrassed."

His eyes narrowed. "I embarrass you?"

"Oliver—*Everything* embarrasses me. I embarrass *myself*." He was determined to take everything I said the wrong way, wasn't he? If only he knew what it was like to be me. How exhausting it was to worry about everything. To worry about this here and now. I had reason to now, though, what with him taking words out of my mouth.

His eyes narrowed another fraction. He pushed against the table, chair rocking back on two feet. "You're no different than anyone else." He crossed his arms over his chest, chair still rocking precariously. What if he fell? "You get what you want and that's all that matters." *It isn't.* I wanted to say so, but his glaring left me tongue-tied. Also embarrassed, but that was this entire situation. "Screw my feelings on the subject." He sounded so bloody *bitter*. But what could I do about it?

"You have no idea, Oliver, what it's like being me," I said in a low voice.

"No." His chair slammed back down and he pointed an accusing finger at me. "You have no idea what it's like being *me*." The colour of his eyes darkened as he got angrier. "What it's like being walked over by *everyone*. You have absolutely no fucking idea."

He stood, hands braced against the table.

I stared up at him, unable to come up with anything to say that would appease him, that would calm him down. My face was burning too, I was pretty sure the whole room could hear him talking. He was doing it on purpose, I could tell, not being quiet.

"I've lost my appetite." He pushed away from the table and stalked over the floor towards the doors.

I stared after him, taken aback. He just *left* me here? I was frozen to my seat. Didn't dare glance around to see the way people must be looking at me.

My whole body tingled, and not the good kind either. The anxiety wound me tight. It wrapped around me, like a blanket, tucking me in, choking me.

I just managed to catch my chair before it fell to the floor. "I'm sorry," I muttered to the waitress as I hurried past her, following after Oliver outside. I looked both ways for him, but had to run to the corner before I saw him. He was heading back up the way we'd come.

I wanted to shout after him, to get him to stop, to try and explain. To make him understand. But I couldn't. I couldn't shout. Shouting was beyond me, it always had been. Raising my voice — no.

I followed him at my own pace. Not because I was actively following *him*, but because that was my way home. Wherever he was headed... I had no idea where he lived. He had walked with me almost all the way up to the blocks the day we got our tests done, though.

The shopping centre came up on our sides, and once we got to the top of the hill, Rokken — the student house — was there. The café was open, as was the shopping centre. Oliver was past the sliding doors leading inside, heading past the windows of Rokken now, while I was only at the corner still.

"Oliver!"

The loud shriek came from a woman stumbling her way out of the sliding doors. She had two bags in her hands — both from *Vinmonopolet*. The only shop where you could buy heavy liquor.

"Oliver!" Another shrilling shriek. She just barely managed to keep herself on her feet.

Oliver had kept walking after her first shout, but he couldn't ignore the second. I could see how his shoulders tensed as he stopped, as he turned, as his focus fell on her. "What?" His voice was flat, resigned, lifeless. I didn't like that voice—even when he'd been yelling at me earlier was better than this.

There didn't seem to be anything in particular she wanted of him though. She stood there, swaying, bottles clinking in both of her bags. Her hair, as blonde as his, was tangled, as if she hadn't combed it today. Or for a week. Her loose-fitting jeans were stained, her trainers were dirty, and she only wore a thin jacket—and it was open too. At least she had a scarf around her neck. It must help some, at least.

"What do you want?" Oliver shouted all of a sudden, startling both me and her. And I wasn't even standing in front of him, with all his focus on me.

"Oliver—"

"Stop it!" He took a step back. "Stop ruining my *life*!"

People were walking both ways on the pavement, some coming out from or going in the sliding doors. Everyone looked at them, though neither Oliver nor his mother—because that's who she had to be right?—seemed to notice any of them.

She swayed some more and then—though

apparently standing upright with nothing in her way — she tripped over her own feet and crashed to the ground. Both her bags hit the concrete hard, alcohol splashing from them, much of it soaking into her already stained jeans.

Oliver hid his face in his hands. "Brilliant. Just brilliant." He rubbed his face. I couldn't tell if he was angry or fighting tears. I didn't know him well enough to say. "What's that — a week's worth of dinner? Two weeks? Down the bloody drain!"

He didn't make a move to help her, and she just sat there on the pavement, amidst the alcohol. "Oliver, honey — "

"Don't!" He took another step back. "I can't pay for food for both of us, Mum. I stayed back here to live with you, to help you, but that means I don't get student loans. I only get a small stipend and it's *not enough*. I'm hungry, Mum, I want to be able to eat for the rest of the month!" He cast a disgusted look down at the mess she'd made, then turned away.

"Oliver!" She shrieked again. "Don't you dare walk away from me! I'm your mother!"

He stopped again, back rigid. "Mothers don't need their sons to care for them. They can take care of themselves." He started walking again, past the windows of the Rokken Café, but he paused once he reached the wall next to them. The wall he'd been leaning on, drunk off his arse, last night.

He drew a shuddering breath, forehead hitting the cold, hard surface.

I hurried past his mother, who was still sitting on the ground, feeling her bags for—I didn't know what. Anything salvageable, perhaps.

"Oliver." I grabbed his shoulders and squeezed gently. "Hey." He was shaking. Either crying or trying to fight it, I wasn't sure as long as I couldn't see his face.

I felt bad about our fight, especially now after seeing his mum. After seeing what he had to live with. No wonder he was a bit messed up, himself.

"I-I have to get her home." He wiped furiously at his face. Likely to be rid of tears.

"I can help."

His eyes were red, but dry, when he turned to me. "No. But thanks. I appreciate it. I just got to—well, this is between me and her."

I nodded, understanding.

We stood there, facing each other in silence for what must've been a whole minute. He broke the trance by bowing his head and slipping past me, heading back over to his mother who had somehow managed to stagger back on her feet.

"Come on, Mum," I heard him murmur. "Let's go home."

I crossed the road, but once there I stopped to watch him slowly lead her forward. They headed along the pavement, towards the bus station. That must mean he lived over there somewhere, so what in the world had he been doing up by the student blocks? *Maybe he just wanted to spend more time with me?*

A vibration in my pocket caught my attention. I fished my phone out, saw it was Mum. She'd want to know how the concert had gone.

After one last look Oliver's way, I turned to head uphill and answered the phone.

Chapter Eight

I didn't see Oliver again until Wednesday when he dropped into the chair next to me.

I eyed him sideways. He must've been waiting outside for the Literature course to end. He usually tended to show up right before the Language course started with a bunch of his mates.

"Hi, Adrian." He was all smiles.

I hadn't suspected that, after what had happened just a few days ago. I would not have bounced back that quick, but then he was more the type to do so than me. He didn't deal with anxiety either, not as far as I could tell, anyway.

"I'm sorry about Saturday." His hand landed atop mine, squeezing gently. "That was me being a complete drama queen. I'm sorry."

"It's okay." I didn't know what to do with my hand now. Was I supposed to squeeze back? But my palm was against the desk, so that was impossible with his pinning it in place.

"Also, what you saw after—well, don't worry about it. I got it under control."

Under control? It sure hadn't seemed like that. "Is it your place, though, to keep it under control?"

He looked down. "She's my mum. We only got each other. If it's not my place, then whose is it?"

"Someone professional? Who can help her get clean?" I'd never dealt with anyone who was alcoholic, but I had seen enough on the telly and in books. Mum liked to watch all kinds of documentaries or reality shows, and a surprisingly amount of people seemed to struggle with substance abuse.

"She refuses. What am I supposed to do? I can't force her." He retracted his hand and instead put both of his in his lap, twining them together. "Besides, I don't want to talk about it. I've lived with it all my life. It's the way it is."

All his life?

"How old are you?" There, I finally dared ask the question.

He eyed me slyly. "Afraid you've been with someone too young for you?"

"No." I turned my head away, wanting to hide the blush I knew had appeared. "You have to be at least nineteen to be in college."

"True." He leaned in, arm pressing against mine. "I'm twenty-one."

"What year you in?"

"My second. You?"

"Second." Something we had in common then.

"So how old are *you*, Adrian?"

"Twenty-three. Turning twenty-four in a few months." I had not started college right after finishing my general studies. I'd stayed at home, working part-time, and trying to deal with my anxiety. Not that I'd managed that well, considering I was still as anxiety-ridden as ever. *Hah*. Working had definitely been a bad experience for me. *So what am I supposed to do when I'm done studying?* I couldn't be a student all my life.

My anxiety spiked in all situations. But when it came to me on a personal level, that was when things mattered, and that was when I turned into a proper mess of nerves. It was a good thing I liked being by myself, or else I might've had depression to deal with on top of it.

"Almost half-way to thirty then." His elbow perched on the table and his cheek rested in his palm as he studied me. He had a stupid grin on his face.

"Ha. Ha." So funny. *Or at least so he thinks*.

"You got any plans after the lecture?"

I shook my head. "Just going back home."

Like always. I never had plans. After four hours of lectures, of sitting amidst a crowd of people, I craved being on my own. "You can come back with me if you want." Except maybe it wouldn't be so bad to have him there. *Maybe*. Depended on what he was like during class, if he was as annoying and obnoxious as ever. Perhaps I should've waited to extend my invitation to the lecture was over.

"I definitely want that." His gaze didn't leave my face. It made me feel incredibly self-conscious. I couldn't look at him when he stared, so I took in the rest of the room instead. It seemed most of the class had arrived by now — and Oliver's mates kept glancing over their shoulder at him. They'd probably never noticed me before either and were wondering what in the world he was doing sitting with me.

Unless he'd told them about us... *I really hope he hasn't*. Who knew what he could've shared.

The lecturer entered the room, most people told her good afternoon. Beside me, Oliver pulled a notebook out of his shoulder bag as well as a pen. The clock on my laptop switched numbers and it was now fifteen past twelve. Time for the lecture to start.

I'd expected Oliver to pay attention to what went on at the front of the room, but instead he scribbled in his notebook. When he straightened, he slid it over to me.

I cast him a confused glance, then looked down. His handwriting wasn't the best, a scrawly mess I almost couldn't make out. He'd written a list. Of questions.

What's your favourite colour?
Any pets?
Dog person or cat person?
Where're you from?
Favourite sex position?
I blinked. *Really?*

He took my hand, put his pen in it, and folded my fingers around it. The message was loud and clear. *Answer them.* It wasn't like they were deep questions, they didn't even need an entire sentence to answer them.

Blue.
Yes.
Dog.
Five hours from here by bus. Any guesses?
Don't know.

Sex position… Like I'd had enough sex to answer that one. I had told him I'd never had it before, that he was my first.

I slid the book back, pen on top of it. He bent over, scribbling anew. When I got it back, he'd written down his own answers.

Green.
Nope.
Cat.
Here.
Every one!

The last one was definitely not a surprise. I commented so. He gave a silent laugh when he read it, then bent to write some more.

I like you, Adrian. Like, really like you.

I stared at the words, taken aback. I hadn't expected them. I knew my face was red again. My hand shook a bit as I put the pen to paper.

I like you too.

It was the truth. I never could've predicted this though. *Him*, of all people. If someone had told me before that Friday, I would've laughed out loud at the ridiculousness of it all. Now — so soon... I had a hard time imagining what would happen if he walked out of my life.

We didn't know each other, so it was ridiculous. It wasn't like he'd been a huge part of my life this past week. We'd had sex two times — well, three with the shower — but that was it. It was hardly a foundation of anything.

Besides, even if it were... We were too different. It would never work.

Stop worrying.

Two words, written on a paper. They

shouldn't help.

Don't worry about tomorrow when you can live today.

I cast him an askance glance. *Poetic, much?* Well… It was something I'd always had trouble with. I couldn't ever just live in the now, I always worried about the future. What would I do when I finished my bachelor? What kind of job did I want to have? What kind of jobs could I expect to get? How was I supposed to support myself if I couldn't get a job? I didn't want to move back in with my mum when I was that old.

There was always something to worry about. My mind found something, no matter what. And when my head started worrying, it transferred to the rest of my body, making me tense and agitated.

A warm hand covered mine. It was resting flat on the desk, next to my computer, and now Oliver's hand rested atop it. It was roughly the same size as mine, and soft. That hand had been around more private parts of me. It had brought me so much pleasure. His whole body had.

It had a calming effect. I wasn't sure that was what he'd been going for or not. He'd clearly read me well enough to see I worried. Was he able to read me well enough to tell when I needed to be calmed down? Maybe he just wanted to hold my hand. That was more likely.

No one around us paid any attention, even though our hands rested atop the desk for all of them to see. We were in the middle of a lecture, true, but *no one paid attention*.

I could still be invisible to everyone else. Even with *Oliver* at my side, who was definitely *not* invisible. He might as well be now though, he hadn't spoken once since the lecture started. He'd been too focused on me.

I had to say I liked it. I preferred it over him speaking his mind about every single thing during the lecture. I liked him better like this, silent and holding my hand without rambling on.

Maybe we would fit together better than I'd thought. He didn't have a care in the world — or so he seemed — whereas I worried about everything. Maybe he'd have a calming effect on me, like he'd had now by just putting his hand on mine. Maybe I didn't have to take my medicine as often anymore.

It was a nice thought. Not at all realistic, but nice nonetheless.

"We need proper lube."

This utterance came once he'd rolled off me

and now lay on his back. I was the one pressed in-between him and the wall this time around.

"Vaseline is good and all, but it's not at all the same."

I wouldn't know. I'd never had sex with lube. I thought the Vaseline worked fine. It sure slicked us both up good enough to do the deed.

"Hey." His hand flopped over to rest on my stomach. "You're quiet."

"I always am."

"Why?"

"Don't have much to say." Or more like major anxiety about saying something wrong. It was overwhelming at times. I didn't want to push him away.

"Really?" He moved his hand a bit, over my navel and down my treasure trail. "I bet you're thinking about a lot. Why not say it?"

"I can't." I really couldn't.

"And why's that?" He sounded puzzled. I bet he was trying to figure me out and failing exceptionally. Mum always said I was all mysterious since I preferred to listen rather than speak.

Should I tell him? Truth was always best when it came to these things, right? At least then he'd know, and hopefully he wouldn't push my boundaries much. "I have anxiety. Like, real bad at times. I worry about everything. Go to lectures early so I won't have people staring at me as I choose my seat. I can't say anything in class no matter how much I know the answer. How much I want to. My body just—it can't. Sometimes it's so bad I have anxiety attacks. Now those are exhausting."

He was silent. "Huh."

Huh? That was all he had to say? I'd told him something only Mum knew about. Something private. Maybe I had put my foot in my mouth and scared him off anyway. Maybe this wasn't something I should've shared at all. It was too private, perhaps, at least this early in—whatever it was we were.

"So your anxiety protects you. I protect myself by being all happy and chatty. We are polar opposites, aren't we?"

We definitely were. "Yeah."

"It can work, you know." His voice had lowered. So had his hand. His fingers were tangling in my pubic hair. I should get to shaving it, trim it a little. Maybe be rid of it altogether? Or maybe not, that would feel too naked. "There's that saying: opposites attract. It can be good. Opposites can fit together. Like pieces of a puzzle."

"Perhaps." I wasn't quite willing to admit I

agreed. I wouldn't have before, but now... well. We sure did fit together in bed. Maybe he was a bit too talkative for my liking in lectures, but as he'd just said, it was something that protected him.

I reckoned he hadn't had the best childhood. Not if his mum had been an alcoholic for long, anyway. He sure didn't have the best life *now*, taking care of her. It shouldn't be like that. Children shouldn't have to take care of their parents. Not until they got old, anyway. Or sick. Alcoholism... sure, it was a sickness, but it was something the alcoholic could do something about. They could get clean, if they got professional help and truly went all in for it.

"How are your parents?"

It was like he'd read my mind. "It's just my mum, mostly. I don't have much to do with my dad, he lives up north with his new family. But Mum's amazing. Been there for me all along. Still is."

"That sounds nice." He turned on his side, and put his head on my shoulder. "Must be nice to have someone like that."

So he hadn't. "What about your mates?"

"They're not close mates, if that's what you're thinking. They're students, we go out partying together. They have no idea I'm even from here. I don't tend to advertise it. They've never met Mum. I just let them think I'm a student from somewhere else, like most of the others. Who stays behind in their hometown anyway? It's pathetic."

"I think it's great you look out for your mum. But, I still think you should think a bit about yourself. Do what you want."

"I wanted to go down to Oslo. Start at the Bårder Academy. Study musical theatre."

Musical theatre? My eyebrows rose in surprise. That must mean he had a good singing voice. Who would take an education that required singing if they couldn't sing, right?

"Did you know we're not supposed to have sex after taking an HIV test? Until you get the results back, anyway. It's not safe."

"No, I did not know that." How was I supposed to? "Where'd you hear that?"

"I read it in a brochure at the clinic."

I frowned. "When did you read a brochure?"

"Well, I didn't read it there. I took it home with me."

I hadn't noticed any brochures—or him taking one.

"But then we've been using condoms since, so I shouldn't think it would be a problem." He scratched his chest thoughtfully.

I certainly hoped not.

Only… "In the shower. We didn't use condoms then." He'd swallowed and I'd— well, I'd swallowed *some*. Most of it had been spit out, but I'd had it in my mouth.

"There's very little chance of contracting an STD from a blowjob." His hand waved carelessly in the air.

I frowned. "It happens. It *can* happen." I'd seen it on *Embarrassing Bodies*. They'd warned about that. You could have it in your throat without even knowing it. That might possibly have been syphilis though… was that an STD that was prevalent in Norway, even? It existed, for sure. With my luck though, that was what I'd get if I ever did get an STD. I would get it—and I wouldn't even know about it.

Something started vibrating on the floor. Oliver leaned over the edge of the bed and came up with his phone. "Hello? Yes, this is him."

I stared at the ceiling as he answered, not wanting to eavesdrop, but not having much of a choice as he was stretched out and pressed against me.

"Oh, really? Yeah—that's great news—yes, thank you! Bye!"

He dropped the phone back on the floor. Since it didn't make much of a sound, I reckoned he'd dropped it atop his clothes. Or mine. Whichever.

"Know who that was?" He propped up on his elbow to look down at me. I shook my head as much as I was able lying on the pillow. "It was the clinic. I'm in the clear." He grinned happily.

I bit my lip.

"Hey, don't worry." He stroked his hand over my shoulder, down my chest. "If it was your first time and I'm clear, then you definitely are."

I hoped so.

There was vibration on the floor again.

"I should think that's yours." Oliver rolled over to his other side and leaned over to rummage in our clothes. His back, and his bum, was on display for me to ogle. And I did. I took full advantage of the view. I didn't even feel embarrassed about it for once.

He threw my phone at me once he'd found it.

I hurried to answer so they wouldn't hang up before I got to it. "Hello?"

A woman spoke softly in my ear, saying my name, wanting to know it was me. It was, obviously. I waited, holding my breath, as she paused. I heard papers rustling, then the news were delivered — "The results were negative."

It was like a great big weight lifted from my stomach. I hadn't even realised the anxiety I'd been carrying around, not that it was this much of it, till it all seemed to just melt away.

I hung up.

Oliver watched me curiously. A little worried too.

I met his gaze. A smile spread slowly on his lips, uncertain. I smiled back. "I'm in the clear too."

He made a whooping sound—then leaned down to kiss me.

I kissed him back a lot more enthusiastically than I'd done the other times we'd kissed.

Negative results on the HIV test, a bloke I actually liked being around—eventually—and lots of sex to be had with said bloke. Good sex. Awesome sex. Good kissing too. And my anxiety had let up a bit, enough for me to be a bit more involved in our activities. It was glorious.

I had absolutely nothing to complain about.

Life was quite grand, actually.

Who would've thought so just a couple of weeks ago?

About TT Kove

TT lives in Norway and writes about gay men living in Norway. She also occasionally writes about gay men living in the UK, because she loves the UK. Norway might be too cold for her, but TT doesn't like the summer, so she's learned to adapt. TT is happiest in front of her computer, creating emotional stories about men loving other men.

Website: www.ttkove.com
E-mail: ttkove@gmail.com
Twitter: www.twitter.com/ttkove
Goodreads:
https://www.goodreads.com/author/show/5035387.T_T_Kove
Pinterest: www.pinterest.com/ttkove/

TT also has a newsletter that she sends out with information about new releases, writing progress, as well as first look on covers, and free books for an honest review: bit.ly/1bMYawk.

Also by TT Kove

ARCTIC LOVE
Polar Nights * Northern Lights * Midnight Sun * White Nights

How About a Boyfriend?

LEGEND & LORE
Forest of Fenris * Desert Fire * The Huntress

MORE THAN ANYTHING
More Than Anything * More Than Words

Protection

SCARRED SOULS
Scarred Souls * Inked Souls

SEASONAL LOVE
Winter Love * Sakura Kiss * Moscow Nights

Summer Fever

Printed in Great Britain
by Amazon